Trouble at
Trident Academy

Battle of the
Best Friends

★ Also by ★

Debbie Dadey

Mermaid Tales

Book 3: *A Whale of a Tale*

Book 4: *Danger in the Deep Blue Sea*

Book 5: *The Lost Princess*

Book 6: *The Secret Sea Horse*

Book 7: *Dream of the Blue Turtle*

Book 8: *Treasure in Trident City*

Book 9: *A Royal Tea*

Book 10: *A Tale of Two Sisters*

Book 11: *The Polar Bear Express*

Book 12: *Wish upon a Starfish*

Book 13: *The Crook and the Crown*

Book 14: *Twist and Shout*

Book 15: *Books vs. Looks*

Book 16: *Flower Girl Dreams*

Book 17: *Ready, Set, Goal!*

Book 18: *Fairy Chase*

Coming Soon

Book 19: *The Narwhal Mystery*

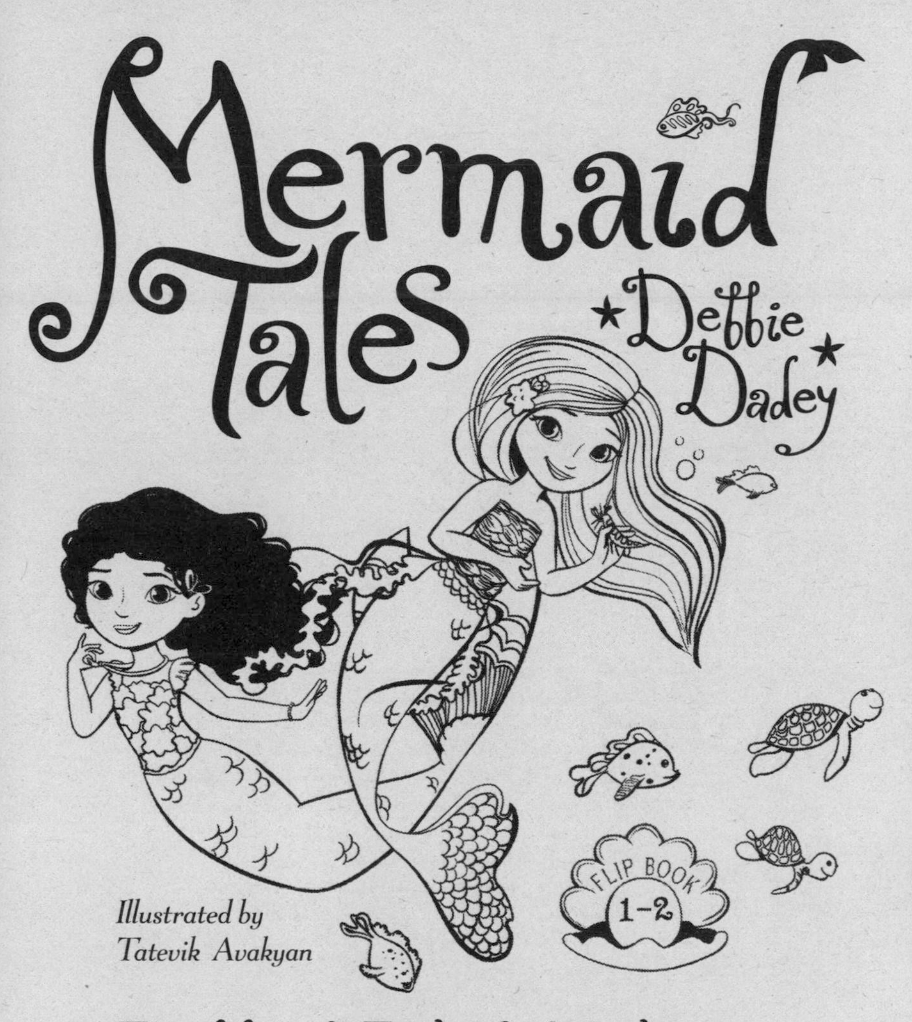

Illustrated by
Tatevik Avakyan

Trouble at Trident Academy
Battle of the Best Friends

ALADDIN
NEW YORK LONDON TORONTO SYDNEY NEW DELHI

ALADDIN
An imprint of Simon & Schuster Children's Publishing Division
1230 Avenue of the Americas, New York, NY 10020
This Aladdin paperback edition August 2018

For information about special discounts for bulk purchases, please contact Simon & Schuster
Special Sales at 1-866-506-1949 or business@simonandschuster.com.
The Simon & Schuster Speakers Bureau can bring authors to your live event.
For more information or to book an event contact the Simon & Schuster Speakers Bureau
at 1-866-248-3049 or visit our website at www.simonspeakers.com.
Designed by Karin Paprocki
The text of this book was set in Belucian Book.
Manufactured in the United States of America 0718 OFF
2 4 6 8 10 9 7 5 3 1
Library of Congress Control Number 2017958370
ISBN 978-1-5344-2857-7 (pbk)
ISBN 978-1-4424-2981-9 (*Trouble at Trident Academy* eBook)
ISBN 978-1-4424-2983-3 (*Battle of the Best Friends* eBook)
These titles were previously published individually.

Trouble at Trident Academy

To my wonderful family:
Eric, Nathan, Becky, and Alex.
I look forward to many
more ocean trips together!

★ ★ ★ ★

Acknowledgments

Thanks to Fiona Simpson, Karen Nagel, and Bethany Buck for letting me swim with the mermaids!

N
E
W
S
The Mayor's House
Pearl's Home
Trident School for Languages
Trident City Hall
Big Rock Cafe
Trident Academy
Trident Plaza Hotel
The Coral Reef
56
Reef 56 Hotel
Merlin's
Angel Fish Antiques

Kelp Fields
Echo's House
People Museum * Shelly's Home
Manta Ray Station
Reef's Fish Store
MerPark
Little V
Whale Mountain
Big V
Trident City

Cast of Characters
Shelly
Echo
Kiki
Pearl
Rocky

Contents

1 Trident Academy

"I CAN'T BELIEVE IT!" ECHO SAID. "IT'S finally happening."

Shelly took a small sip of her sea-weed juice before pushing a lock of red hair from her face. Usually she didn't care if her hair stuck straight up, but today was special. "We're so lucky to get an invitation to Trident Academy. I didn't think it would happen to me."

Echo and Shelly both lived in Trident City, not far from the famous Trident Academy. They had been friends since they'd played together in the small-fry area of MerPark. The eight-year-old mermaids were celebrating their first day of school with breakfast at the Big Rock Café, a favorite hangout. The place was packed with students proudly wearing their Trident Academy sashes. The two mergirls didn't see a third mergirl swimming up behind them. Her name was Pearl. Echo and Shelly usually tried to avoid the bossy mergirl from their neighborhood.

"Oh my Neptune!" Pearl snapped when

she saw Shelly. "I can't believe *you*, of all merpeople, got into Trident." Usually only very wealthy or extremely smart students were accepted. Pearl was rich. Echo was a quick learner. Shelly was neither, but she knew more about ocean animals than both of them put together.

Echo came to her friend's defense. "Of course Shelly got into Trident. She is very talented."

"At *what*?" Pearl asked. "Digging for crabs?"

Shelly glanced at her dirty fingernails and immediately hid them under her blue tail fin. "At least I know *how* to hunt crabs. I bet you'd starve to death if you had to do something for yourself."

Pearl flipped her blond hair, stuck her pointy nose up in the water, and said, "I know how to do plenty of things."

"Name one," Shelly said.

"How to be on time for school, for starters," she said. Pearl spun around and flicked her gold tail, knocking seaweed juice all over Shelly's new Trident sash!

Splash!

Pearl giggled and swam off toward school.

"Oh no!" Shelly squealed, dabbing green juice off the gold-and-blue sash. "She did that on purpose!"

Echo glared after Pearl before helping her friend wipe the sash. "It's fine now. You can hardly see it," Echo said. That wasn't *exactly* true—there was definitely a green blob on Shelly's sash.

"We'd better get going," Echo said, adjusting the glittering plankton bow in her dark curly hair. "We don't want to be late on our first day."

Shelly groaned. She wasn't quite so excited now. "If Trident Academy is filled with merpeople like Pearl, then I don't think I'm going to like it."

"There's only one way to find out," Echo said, taking a deep breath. "Let's go."

2

Burps

WOW," SHELLY SAID, staring up at the ceiling of the huge clamshell. "This is amazing." Only a few shells in the ocean had ever grown as large as Trident Academy. The front hall alone could fit a humpback whale, and the ceiling was filled with colorful old carvings that showed the history of the merpeople.

"It's awesome, but we'd better get to class," Echo said, grabbing Shelly's elbow. "Third graders are down this way." Echo's older sister went to Trident Academy, so Echo already knew a lot about the school.

Shelly didn't think she'd ever seen so many merpeople in one place. Hundreds of students swam quickly through the massive shell, looking for their classrooms. Each wore a different-colored sash for their grade, from third to tenth.

"Here's our room," Echo said. She shoved aside a seaweed curtain and disappeared inside.

Shelly gulped and followed her friend.

She hoped Pearl wouldn't be in their classroom, but as she entered the class . . .

"Oh no. Did a stinkfish just swim in?" Pearl snapped as she sat at a rock desk.

"No," said a merboy with a big head. "But a burpfish did." He let out a big, long burp right in Pearl's face.

"That is so disgusting, Rocky," Pearl said. "Didn't your parents teach you any manners?"

"I'll tell you what's really disgusting," Rocky said. "That jewelry you're wearing."

Pearl shook her head. "My pearls are *sooooo* beautiful." She ran her fingers over the long necklace.

"Actually," a tiny, dark-haired mergirl said, "pearls *are* sort of disgusting. They're made when an oyster or mussel secretes nacre around an irritant."

Pearl sniffed at the tiny mergirl. "So what?"

"Secretes?" another merboy asked. "What's that?"

"Kind of like spitting," the mergirl explained.

"I knew that," Rocky said with a grin. "That means she's wearing puke around her neck." Several merboys and mergirls in the class giggled at the joke.

The small mergirl nodded, and Shelly took a closer look at her. She had long black hair that reached all the way to her tail; wide, dark eyes; and the palest of skin. Her mertail was a brilliant purple, unlike any Shelly'd ever seen. Shelly's own tail was blue, and Echo's was pink. The mergirl with the purple tail didn't look even a little bit afraid of Pearl. Anyone who could stand up to Pearl was awesome. Shelly knew she was going to like this mergirl.

"Watch this!" Rocky said. He spit into the water around Pearl. At that moment a tall, thin teacher with green hair and a white tail swam into the room. "Young merboy," she asked, "*what* are you doing?"

Rocky grinned. "I'm . . . I'm . . . I'm seeing if I can turn her into a giant glob of spit."

Shelly hid a giggle. She was pretty sure she liked Rocky, too. Maybe Trident Academy wouldn't be so bad after all.

3
Mrs. Karp

"GOOD MORNING, STUDENTS. Welcome to Trident Academy. My name is Mrs. Karp," said their teacher. "I will be teaching you reading, storytelling, and science. I trust your parents have started your education and we'll be able to move along quickly."

Shelly squirmed in her sponge seat. Her parents had died when she was just a small fry, and she lived with her grandfather in an apartment above the People Museum. She hoped he'd taught her all she needed to know, since Trident Academy expected their students to have been home-schooled for two years.

All merkids were taught at home until third grade. Sometimes her grandfather was a little forgetful, and some days he hadn't remembered about Shelly's lessons. And Shelly hadn't reminded him. She'd much rather explore underwater caves or play with sea turtles than sit still for lessons.

"Mr. Bottom will teach you math,

life-saving, and astronomy," Mrs. Karp continued.

Rocky snickered at the name Mr. Bottom, but Mrs. Karp silenced him with a glare. "Trident Academy is lucky to have other special teachers that you'll meet later this week. Today we will get to know each other better and start your first project."

Pearl gasped and raised her hand. "What do we have to do?"

Mrs. Karp smiled at the classroom of twenty mergirls and merboys. "I'm glad you are eager to get right to your studies. Your first assignment at Trident Academy will be a report on krill and shrimp."

Shelly groaned quietly. There were so

many exciting things to learn about, like the dolphins and whales she wanted to swim with. Why did they have to learn about silly little shrimp?

"As you know, many sea creatures, including us, would not live long without krill to eat. Why, even humans are known to eat krill, especially those who live near Kiki's far-off waters." Mrs. Karp nodded toward the mergirl who had stood up to Pearl.

Far-off waters? Shelly thought. She was even more curious about Kiki now.

"You will need to collect at least four types of krill or shrimp and complete a seaweed and octopus-ink study on each of them." Merkids used orange sea pens with their sharpened ends dipped in octopus ink to write on neatly cut pieces of seaweed for their studies.

"How many pieces of seaweed?" asked a large mergirl in the back of the room.

"At least one per krill or shrimp," answered Mrs. Karp.

Groans came from throughout the class. "The wise merstudent will start right away," Mrs. Karp told them. "In fact, we will go to the library until lunchtime so you may begin your reports."

Echo leaned over to Shelly. "Want to work together?" she asked.

Shelly nodded. This was their first

project for Trident Academy. She didn't want to mess it up.

As they floated down the hall toward the school library, Echo pointed to the Trident Academy message board. There were notices posted all over it, inviting students to join different clubs.

Shelly noticed a sign written in big green letters:

SHELL WARS PRACTICE
AFTER SCHOOL TODAY
IN MERPARK

Shelly smiled. Shell Wars! She loved playing Shell Wars. Maybe she could make the school team! The rush of water around her face when she scored a goal was a lot more exciting than learning about krill. In her mind, she was already smacking a shell around.

"I want to be one of those," Echo said, pointing to a message about the Tail Flippers, a group that cheered for sporting events.

Shelly nodded. "That looks great. But I think I'll try out for Shell Wars."

"Me too," Kiki said from behind them, and Shelly gave her a big smile.

Pearl swam up beside the mergirls. "Shell Wars is disgusting. I'd never try out for anything so rough."

Shelly and Echo ignored Pearl as they passed a dark gray merman with a huge frown on his face. He looked so sad, Shelly felt like crying. "Who is that?" she whispered.

"I bet that's Mr. Fangtooth," Echo whispered back. "My sister told me all about him. He works in the cafeteria."

"I heard he's a grouch," Pearl said, "and he hasn't smiled in forty years."

"Maybe he just needs cheering up," Shelly said, immediately feeling sorry for Mr. Fangtooth. "I bet Echo and I could make him smile."

"Okay," Pearl said. "It's a bet."

4

The Bet

IF YOU WERE GRUMPY, WHAT WOULD cheer you up?" Shelly asked Echo as they ate their lunch later that day.

Echo thought about it for a few minutes. "If I found something human," she admitted.

Shelly sighed. She didn't understand her friend's fascination with anything that had to do with humans. Shelly thought killer whales were much more interesting.

Echo swallowed a handful of tiny octopus legs before licking her fingers. "Maybe we could try making funny faces at Mr. Fangtooth. That always makes my dad smile."

Shelly grinned. "What a great idea. Let's put our lunch trays away and make faces at him."

Echo and Shelly stood at the service window of the cafeteria kitchen. Shelly crossed her blue eyes and pushed her nose up against it to look like a dog fish. Echo pulled her dark hair into tall points and puffed her cheeks out. Mr. Fangtooth frowned at them.

Echo blew out the air in her cheeks, making lots of little bubbles. "Why didn't he smile?" she whispered. "That always works with my dad."

"I have the feeling that Mr. Fangtooth hasn't smiled in a very, very long time. I think we're going to have to do something drastic," Shelly said.

"Like what?" Echo asked.

Shelly shrugged and looked around the cafeteria at the scenes of merfolk history carved on the walls. Merstudents of all ages talked and ate their school lunches at polished granite tables with the gold Trident Academy logo in their centers.

Shelly saw Kiki sitting with Pearl and a group of mergirls. Kiki smiled at Shelly, and Shelly gave a little wave, wishing she had thought to invite Kiki to sit with them. Then she turned back to Mr. Fangtooth.

Mr. Fangtooth made a horrible face and bellowed at the mergirls. *Roar!*

Echo screamed and fell right into Rocky. His plate of ribbon worms flew onto Echo's hair.

"*Eeewww!* Get them off!" Echo squealed. Shelly quickly began pulling the long, thin, black-and-white worms out of Echo's curly hair. She stopped when she heard a booming sound.

It was Mr. Fangtooth! His laughter rocked the cafeteria.

All the students looked up from their lunches to see what was happening. Pearl glared at Shelly. "See?" Shelly said. "I told you we could make Mr. Fangtooth laugh. We win the bet!"

Pearl opened her mouth, but she didn't get the chance to talk because Headmaster Hermit's voice came over the conch shell: "Shelly Siren and Echo Reef, please report to the headmaster's office immediately."

"Ooooh," Rocky teased. "You're in big trouble now."

Shelly gulped. It was only her first day at Trident Academy. Now she was worried it would also be her last.

Disaster

"IT WAS HORRIBLE," ECHO TOLD HER older sister, Crystal, later that afternoon at their shell. "I thought for sure we were going to get kicked out of Trident Academy on our first day!"

Crystal shook her head. "You shouldn't have made faces at Mr. Fangtooth. Then you wouldn't have ended up with worms in your hair. The headmaster has spies everywhere, so you have to behave yourselves."

"We were only trying to cheer up Mr. Fangtooth," Shelly explained.

"You'd better stay out of trouble," Crystal warned.

"That's why I'm here," Shelly said. "We're going to work on our project so we'll get finished early."

"That's great," Crystal said. "I can help you if you'd like."

"That's really nice of—" Shelly started to say.

"But we have something else to do first," Echo interrupted her friend.

Crystal shrugged. "Okay. I have to work at the store soon anyway. Good luck." Crystal and Echo's dad ran Reef's Fish Store, which sold small exotic sea creatures of all kinds. Crystal quickly left, and Shelly worried that her feelings were hurt.

"Maybe we should have let her help," Shelly said.

Echo shook her head. "No, Crystal just wants to boss me around. It's a pain having an older sister."

Shelly was an only child, so she thought it would be great to have a brother or sister.

"Besides," Echo said, "I want to show you what I can do." She did a huge backward flip and twisted to the left and right.

"Watch out!" Shelly yelled, and fell sideways, knocking a beautiful glass vase off a turtle shell table. The vase broke into a million pieces.

Echo's tail did even more damage. She whacked three glowing jellyfish lamps, which rolled across the room. The jellyfish shrugged at Echo and swam out of the shell. Once they left, Echo's living room got much darker. The only light came from a row of shining plankton that lined the bottom of the shell.

"Oh, I'm so sorry," Shelly said. "I didn't mean to break your vase. Echo, I can't do anything right. I should just quit everything, including Trident Academy. I know I won't be able to do all the projects, and I sure won't be able to make the Shell Wars team."

Echo swam through the darkened room to grab her friend by the arm. "Don't be silly. I was the one who caused this disaster. It was all because I wanted to practice for Tail Flippers."

"You did a great flip," Shelly admitted. "You just needed more room." Shelly was right. Echo's shell was full of people-junk that she'd collected.

But Echo shook her head. "There's another problem," she said.

"What's that?" Shelly asked. "I'm sure you'll make the team."

Echo slowly lifted her pink tail so her friend could see. A huge black pot was stuck on the bottom. "Help me get it off, Shelly. I can't go to Trident Academy with this on my tail!"

Shelly tried hard not to laugh as she helped her friend. She pulled. She tugged. She smacked the pot with her own tail. Shelly poured kelp oil into the pot and tugged even harder. Nothing worked. The pot was stuck fast on Echo's tail.

Echo started crying. "What am I going to do?"

Merbrats

THE NEXT MORNING, SHELLY sped through the water. She hurried past an older merwoman, who raised her fist in disgust. "Young merbrats think they can just knock over anyone in their way."

"So sorry!" Shelly apologized to the

woman, who had only been splashed a bit. "I can't be late."

"Rush, rush, rush," the old merwoman complained. "Why is everyone in such a big hurry, anyway?"

It was almost time for their second day of school. Shelly had to find out if Echo's parents had been able to remove the pot from her tail. Echo had been so upset yesterday, they hadn't even worked on their krill project, and Shelly was worried they were going to be behind the rest of the class.

She was meeting Echo outside her shell so they could swim to school together. Hopefully the pot was gone and nothing else would go wrong! But when Shelly arrived, Echo's red eyes told her everything.

"They couldn't get it off! This is the worst thing that could have happened to me."

Shelly hugged her friend. She didn't think a pot on her tail was the *worst* that could happen, but it *was* pretty bad. "Maybe you could put something over it?" she suggested.

Echo thought for a moment, then smiled. "That's a great idea. Maybe this will work." She reached into a pile near her front door and pulled out a piece of glittery material.

"What's that?" Shelly asked.

"I found it last week. My dad said he thought it was called 'cloth.' People wear it," Echo explained as she wrapped the sparkly material around her tail *and* the black pot.

Shelly rolled her eyes. More people stuff! She thought shells and woven seaweed made perfectly fine clothing, but she had to admit, the sparkly cloth looked pretty. "You look fabulous!" she told Echo.

"Really?"

"Pearl will probably be jealous," Shelly said. "Now let's hurry or we'll be late." It was hard for Echo to swim fast with her tail all wrapped up, so Shelly pulled her along. They made it to school just as the conch horn sounded.

In class, Mrs. Karp held up a small, almost-see-through creature. "Who can tell me what this is?"

Rocky's hand shot up immediately, and Mrs. Karp nodded toward him. "Lunch!" he exclaimed.

Mrs. Karp frowned and nodded at Pearl. "That is an Antarctic krill," Pearl said smugly. "It is the main food of the blue whale."

Mrs. Karp pointed at Kiki. "Can you add anything to Pearl's explanation?"

Kiki stood on her tail and spouted off information. "Krill are shrimplike crustaceans that form a large part of the zooplankton and our food chain."

"What did she say?" Rocky asked. "What's a zooplankton?"

Shelly wondered the same thing, but Mrs. Karp continued with the lesson.

"Very good," Mrs. Karp told Kiki. "Now, who can pick out other crustaceans from this aquarium?" Mrs. Karp tapped a glass box that was filled with different sea creatures. Shelly knew about most large sea life, but she wasn't sure what a crustacean was, so she looked down at her tail. When no one raised their hand, Mrs. Karp called on Echo.

Oh no, thought Shelly. She was afraid the other merkids would tease Echo if they saw the pot. She held her breath as Echo floated to the front of the room. "Look at her tail," several students whispered as Echo swam by.

But then Kiki said, "It's so pretty."

Another girl named Morgan added, "And so shiny."

Shelly relaxed. Everyone liked Echo's cloth. Everything was going to be fine. But then Echo's tail banged on the teacher's marble desk. *Boing!* The pot made a horrible noise.

"Echo has a musical tail!" a boy named Adam yelled. The class laughed, and Echo's face turned bright red. For a terrible moment Shelly thought that Echo would rush away, but thankfully Mrs. Karp silenced the class.

The rest of the morning was pretty

uneventful until lunchtime. All the mer-girls in the class swarmed around Echo. "Where did you get that? What's it called?" one asked.

Echo smiled and patiently answered all their questions, but she ate lunch with just Shelly. "Whew, I'm glad they didn't see the pot," Echo whispered.

In fact, Echo made it through the rest of the day without any problems.

AFTER SCHOOL ON THE WAY TO MERPARK, Shelly told Echo, "If you don't mind waiting, I'll help you swim home after Shell Wars practice."

"Thanks," Echo said. "If I can't try out for Tail Flippers, at least I can cheer you on."

Shelly felt bad. It didn't seem fair for her to try out for Shell Wars if Echo couldn't be a Tail Flipper. Maybe she should sit with Echo instead of practicing. Shelly started to tell her friend that she'd changed her mind about trying out, but then she had an idea. If her plan worked, it would solve everything.

Harlequin Shrimp

"DID YOU SEE THAT?" SHELLY asked Echo. The two mergirls were swimming over to Shelly's home after Shell Wars practice. Actually, Shelly swam slowly and pulled Echo along.

"I think that's a harlequin shrimp," Echo said, pointing to a blue-and-white-spotted creature. "It's just like the picture in the dictionary. Quick, catch it for our report!"

Shelly did hurry, but she wasn't fast enough. Rocky came out of nowhere and snatched up the shrimp, along with the starfish it was eating.

"Hey, that was ours!" Shelly complained.

Rocky laughed and swam off with the bright blue-and-white shrimp. "Not anymore."

Shelly wanted to chase him, but she swam back to where Echo waited.

"Did you get it?" Echo asked.

"No," Shelly answered. "Rocky did."

"I used to think he was cute, but not now," Echo said.

Shelly giggled. "Who? The harlequin shrimp or Rocky?" she teased.

Echo laughed. "Rocky, silly."

"You thought Rocky was cute?" Shelly asked.

"A little bit," Echo said with a shrug.

"Let's go," Shelly said. "But keep your eyes open for sea cucumbers. Mrs. Karp told me that emperor shrimp live on them. The more shrimp we collect, the better grade we'll get."

The friends looked for specimens. They saw a hammerhead shark's shadow and huge vent tube worms, but no shrimp or krill.

"Look over there," Echo said.

"Is it an emperor shrimp?" Shelly asked.

"No, it's Mr. Fangtooth," Echo whispered. The mergirls hid behind a merstatue as Mr. Fangtooth wiggled toward the Big Rock Café. Through the open windows they watched as he sat at a table by himself, and a merwaitress brought him food.

"He looks so sad," Echo said, peeking around the merstatue.

"Maybe he doesn't have a family to cheer him up," Shelly said. She was grateful she had her grandfather.

"At least we got him to smile yesterday," Echo said.

"And we were sent to the headmaster's office for it," Shelly reminded her.

Echo nodded. "Still, maybe we could make him smile again, and keep him smiling."

"That'd be nice, as long as we don't get in trouble," Shelly said. "I like Mr. Fangtooth a whole lot better than I like Pearl."

"Pearl was bragging about how great

her report was going to be," Echo said. "I don't think it's nice to brag."

"It isn't," Shelly said. "But we'd better get to work on our reports. Let's go to my house." Shelly didn't tell Echo about her plan, but she secretly hoped her grandfather could get the pot off Echo's tail.

"Maybe your grandfather can help us with our reports," Echo said.

Shelly shook her head. "No, we have to do it on our own." If Echo wouldn't let her sister help, why should they ask Shelly's grandfather?

"I bet your grandfather would like to help with our schoolwork," Echo said.

"Sure he would," Shelly said. "But we should do this without him."

"Why?" Echo asked. "He's really smart. And we could get a good grade."

Shelly rolled her eyes. Her whole life, people had been telling her how amazing her grandfather was. She loved her grandfather, but she liked doing things on her own. "No, I don't want to ask him."

Echo put her right hand on her right hip and banged the pot on the seafloor. "Well, I want to."

Shelly scrunched up her nose. Usually she agreed with Echo, but just then she was tired and grouchy. "Well, I don't."

"I do!" Echo yelled.

"I don't!" Shelly yelled back.

"Then I don't want to work with you!" Echo shouted.

"Then I don't want to work with you, either!" Shelly shouted back.

Echo swam away as fast as she could with the pot on her tail. *Bump. Bump. Bump.* The pot thumped along the ocean floor.

Shelly wanted to swim after her friend and tell her she was sorry. But she didn't. "I never even got to tell her my plan," Shelly said to herself. She had the horrible feeling that she'd never be friends with Echo again.

8

Pearl

"I DON'T BELIEVE IT!" SHELLY GASPED. It was the next morning. She had decided to stop by Echo's shell to apologize and help her friend get to school. But Echo wasn't alone. *Pearl* was holding Echo's hand and helping her. Tied around Pearl's tail was a smaller, but still sparkling, piece of cloth just like Echo's. Shelly wondered where Pearl had managed to get the fabric.

Shelly waited behind a kelp plant in MerPark to let Echo and Pearl pass. "I have only one page finished for my report," Echo admitted.

"I haven't started yet," Pearl said.

"You haven't?" Echo asked.

"No, but I'm not worried," Pearl said. "My dad promised to get me some shrimp. And if I were you, I'd just get your father to bring some home from his store. Reef's has tons of shrimp and krill."

"I never thought about that," Echo said.

"You'd be silly not to ask him for help," Pearl said. "It'd be so easy."

Echo nodded. "Maybe. My dad does have lots of neat shrimp, but I don't know if he would give me any."

"You could take them when he wasn't looking," Pearl said.

"That would be stealing!" Echo said.

"No, it wouldn't. It's your store too, isn't it?" Pearl asked.

Echo frowned. "I guess you are right."

"Of course I'm right," Pearl said. "Now let's get to Trident Academy."

Shelly watched her best friend swim away with Pearl. When they were out of sight, Shelly floated slowly to school. All she could think about was Pearl teaching Echo how to do terrible things. Somehow Shelly had to find a way to get Echo away from Pearl.

But Pearl sat next to Echo in the library. Pearl sat next to Echo in the lunchroom. Shelly looked to see if Echo wanted to make Mr. Fangtooth laugh, but Echo didn't even glance Shelly's way. Shelly swam over to an empty granite table in the corner and sat by herself.

"Hi," said a small voice. Shelly looked up from her lunch of leftover clam casserole to find Kiki. "May I sit here?" Kiki asked.

"Sure," Shelly said. "How do you like Trident Academy?"

Kiki shrugged and sat down. "It's okay, but I miss my parents and brothers."

"How many brothers do you have?" Shelly asked.

"Seventeen," Kiki said.

"*Seventeen!*" Shelly shrieked. "Are you kidding me?"

Kiki laughed. "No, I really do have seventeen brothers and not one sister."

"I don't have any brothers or sisters, but I'd like some," Shelly told her.

"It's okay, but very noisy. I always thought I wanted to go somewhere quieter, but the dorm rooms at Trident Academy are almost too quiet in the afternoon."

"Wow, you live in the school dorm?" Shelly asked. "That sounds so cool."

Kiki shook her head and whispered, "I have Wanda for a roommate. She snores really loudly."

Shelly laughed, and out of the corner of her eye she saw Echo look at her. Echo frowned and said something to Pearl and the other mergirls at her table. They all looked in Shelly's direction and burst out laughing. Shelly had a terrible feeling they were laughing at her.

AFTER SCHOOL, SHELLY FLOATED OVER to Shell Wars practice. Kiki was already warming up by gently tossing a shell back and forth with a group of merkids. Kiki waved as Shelly took her place on the field.

In Shell Wars, two teams try to shoot a small shell into the other team's treasure chest and whoever scores more goals wins. Each chest is guarded by a goalie, which just happens to be an octopus! The players use long whale bones to slam the shells with all their might! If anyone touches a shell with their hands or body, they're out of the game, so it's important to pay attention.

"Watch out!" Kiki yelled.

Whack! The shell hit Shelly right in the stomach. She hit the ocean floor hard.

"Oh my gosh!" Echo screamed. "Is she hurt?"

"Serves her right," Pearl snapped. "Shell Wars is a gross game. Who wants to play with a dirty old shell?"

"I might not like Shell Wars, but Shelly does, and she's my friend," Echo said, swimming away from Pearl.

"Are you all right?" Echo asked Shelly as she sat up.

Shelly held her stomach, but she smiled. "I am if we're friends again."

"Are we friends again?" Echo asked.

Shelly nodded, and the two mergirls

hugged. Pearl stuck her nose up in the water and swam home alone.

"You want to come over to my house after practice?" Shelly asked Echo.

Echo nodded and giggled. "I'm so glad we're not mad at each other anymore." The friends hugged again before Shelly went back to practice and Echo sat down to watch.

Neither mergirl noticed that Kiki had come over to check on Shelly as well. They didn't see Kiki standing beside them. Neither one noticed when she swam away either. "It's like they ignored me on purpose. I didn't mean to hit Shelly," Kiki whispered. She floated off with tears in her eyes.

A Neat Trick

ECHO WATCHED THE REST OF Shell Wars practice. She had to admit that Shelly was good—probably even better than Rocky, and he boasted that he was the best player in the whole ocean.

"You're awesome," Echo told her friend as the merkids finished scrimmaging and Shelly swam over to the sidelines.

"Thanks. I really hope I can make the team! Now let's go to my shell to work on our projects," Shelly suggested, giving Echo's arm a little tug. As the girls swam by a cluster of sea lilies, they didn't realize that Echo's sparkly cloth was caught. In one quick merminute, it fell off and the teasing began.

"Echo has a pot tail!" yelled Rocky. Several other merboys and mergirls followed Rocky's pointing finger to the black pot still stuck on Echo's tail.

"Pot Tail! Pot Tail!" Rocky called after her.

Shelly wanted to bang the pot on Rocky's

head, but she needed to get Echo away from his teasing, so she swam quickly toward home, pulling Echo with her.

"I'm so embarrassed," Echo said when they were safely inside Shelly's apartment.

"Don't worry about it," Shelly said. "If Pearl had seen it, she'd be wearing a pot on her tail tomorrow too."

Echo wiped away a tear. "Do you really think so?"

Shelly nodded. "She wore a sparkly cloth today, didn't she?"

Echo laughed. "That's right, she did."

"I bet my grandfather can get that pot off," Shelly said, finally glad to be telling Echo her plan.

"That's a great idea!" Echo yelled. "He

is, after all, an expert on human things."

Shelly shrugged. Not only was Echo fascinated with human stuff, but so was Shelly's grandfather. He was the director of the People Museum and knew more than anyone in Trident City about human beings and what went on above the sea. There had been many afternoons when Echo had been content to wander around the museum with Shelly's grandpa, looking at useless human tools. But Shelly had been bored to tears.

"And if he can't get your pot off, then I'll find one to put on my tail so we'll match," Shelly said. "We'll have a pot-tail club."

Echo smiled at her friend. "You are the best merfriend in the whole world."

"Come on, let's go find Grandpa," Shelly said.

GRANDPA SIREN TOOK ONE LOOK AT ECHO'S tail and grinned. "Are you sure you want it off? You never know when a good pot could come in handy."

"Grandpa! She really wants it off," Shelly pleaded.

Grandpa Siren rubbed his chin. "I wonder . . . ," he said as he floated off to his storeroom of extra human gadgets.

Bang! Crash! Bang!

"What's he doing in there?" Echo asked.

Shelly shrugged. Her grandpa came out of the storage area with a large wire basket full of small glass bottles, which

he immediately began searching through.

Echo picked one up labeled DANGER: MOTOR OIL. "Will this help me?" she asked.

Grandpa immediately snatched the bottle away. "It would help, but it would also pollute our water. It's deadly to ocean life."

Echo gulped and backed away from the bottles. Grandpa continued looking until he held one up. "This should do the trick."

He poured the tiniest amount of yellow liquid over Echo's tail, and immediately the water filled with round blobs that bounced off each other. "What *is* this stuff?" Echo asked.

"Vegetable oil," Grandpa explained. "I just applied a drop, but I think it worked."

Echo squealed as the pot slid off her tail.

She gave Grandfather a hug. "You're the greatest!"

"Now we can finish our projects," Shelly said. "And look! You've *already* caught two shrimp." Sure enough, two glowing hinge-beak shrimp floated in the bottom of the pot.

Grandpa raised his furry eyebrows. "Girls, do you need any help with your assignment?"

Shelly looked at Echo. Echo giggled. "No, we're supposed to do it on our own." And that's exactly what the friends did.

AFTER THE GIRLS HAD WORKED FOR several hours, Echo said, "I don't want to go to school tomorrow."

"But our projects are turning out great," Shelly answered. "We even found two snapping shrimp." Shelly almost wished they hadn't found the loud creatures. Their popping noises were driving her crazy.

"I'm afraid the kids will make fun of me," Echo said.

Shelly thought her friend might be right. Even though the pot was finally off Echo's tail, Rocky and Pearl did like to tease, and a pot on a tail was kind of funny. But then Shelly remembered something her grandfather had told her: "Sticks and stones may break my bones, but words will never hurt me."

"But words *do* hurt my feelings sometimes," Echo said.

"They only hurt if you let them," Shelly said. "Just pretend you don't care. If you don't get upset, everyone will stop teasing."

"Will that really work?" Echo asked.

Shelly nodded. "Of course it will." She sure hoped she was right.

Best Merfriend Ever

HEY, POT-TAIL, WHERE'S YOUR pot?" Rocky asked the next morning at school.

"Right here," Echo said, holding up the pot that now held Shelly's and Echo's projects.

Rocky grinned and said, "I liked it better on your tail."

Shelly was surprised and happy that Rocky didn't say another word. Echo had been worried for no reason.

Mrs. Karp splashed her tail sharply, and all the merstudents quickly found their desks. Shelly and Echo proudly turned in their reports, but they couldn't believe their eyes when Kiki turned in at least a dozen seaweed pages and a small chest full of shrimp and krill.

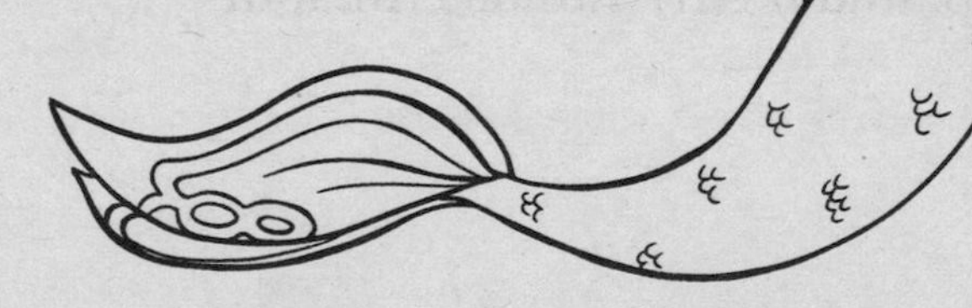

"Wow," Echo whispered. "She must be really smart."

Kiki overheard this as she sat down in her seat. She shrugged. "I'm so sorry I hit you in the stomach at practice yesterday. I felt so bad, I came back to school and worked late on my report."

"It's okay," Shelly said. "I wasn't hurt." Now *she* felt sorry. She hadn't said good-bye to Kiki when she'd left the park yesterday. Shelly hoped she hadn't hurt Kiki's feelings.

Mrs. Karp frowned when Rocky turned in two small seaweed pages with a harlequin shrimp and Pearl handed in four shrimp that clearly had prices marked on their tails.

Pearl swam back to her seat and muttered, "My dad had to work late. He said the project was silly anyway."

Shelly had to admit she'd actually enjoyed working on the project. She'd never known there were so many different kinds of shrimp in the waters around her home.

At lunchtime, Echo and Shelly sat at a table together. Wanda and some other mergirls who boarded at Trident filled up Pearl's table. Many of them wore sparkly cloths tied around their tails.

"See what you started?" Shelly smiled. "Now *everyone's* wearing something glittery around their tails."

"How funny is that?" Echo said with

a giggle. "Maybe something even funnier would make Mr. Fangtooth smile. But what can we do?"

Shelly took a bite of her glasswort sandwich before looking around the lunchroom. She saw Kiki floating over to a small table in the corner. She was going to eat lunch all by herself. "Would you mind if we made someone else smile today?" Shelly asked Echo.

"Who?" Echo asked.

Shelly nodded toward Kiki. "She's new to Trident City, and I think she's a little lonely. Her family lives far away."

The two friends stared at Kiki. She wasn't smiling, and she looked like she'd rather be anyplace but Trident Academy.

Echo smiled. "I told you that you are the best merfriend ever. Let's go sit with her and make her feel at home."

And that's exactly what they did.

SNAPPING SHRIMP

By Shelly Siren

My favorite shrimp is the snapping shrimp, even though it is noisy. It's only the size of my finger, but when its jaws snap shut, it sounds like a hundred merpeople cracking their knuckles. I was lucky to find one, since they usually live in warm, shallow waters.

HARLEQUIN SHRIMP

By Echo Reef

My favorite shrimp is the harlequin shrimp. I like the blue-spotted ones the best, although the purple-, red-, and orange-spotted ones are nice too. The only thing I don't like about harlequin shrimp is that they eat starfish. I like starfish a lot, and I hate to see them hurt.

CLEANER SHRIMP

By Rocky Ridge

Cleaner shrimp are the best because they eat dead stuff out of a fish's mouth. One time I let a cleaner shrimp live in my mouth for a month. I didn't have to brush my teeth until my dad saw it and made me spit it out.

ANEMONE SHRIMP

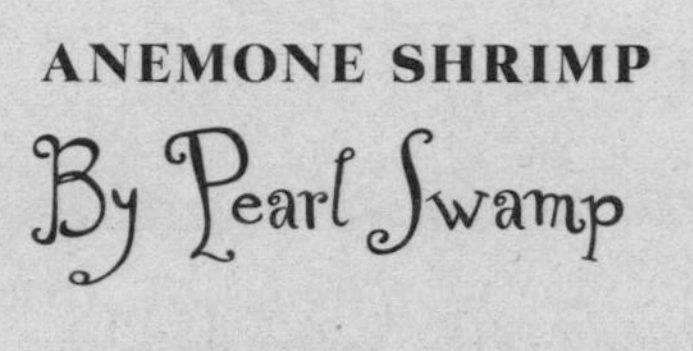

I think all shrimp and krill are disgusting, but if I had to pick a favorite, I would pick the anemone shrimp. I like its purple and white spots because they look a little bit like pearls. This shrimp can live beside an anemone without getting stung.

ANTARCTIC KRILL

By Kiki Coral

I think Antarctic krill are interesting, but I am very worried about them. Because the waters are getting warmer, there are fewer krill. A single blue whale can eat as many as four million krill in a day. What will happen to the whales if the krill disappear? I think merfolk should find out what is making the waters warmer and stop it.

WORDS BY DEBBIE DADEY

REFRAIN:

Let the water roar

Deep down we're swimming along

Twirling, swirling, singing the mermaid song.

VERSE 1:

Shelly flips her tail

Racing, diving, chasing a whale

Twirling, swirling, singing the mermaid song.

VERSE 2:

Pearl likes to shine

Oh my Neptune, she looks so fine

Twirling, swirling, singing the mermaid song.

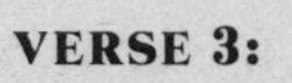

VERSE 3:

Shining Echo flips her tail

Backward and forward without fail

Twirling, swirling, singing the mermaid song.

VERSE 4:

Amazing Kiki

Far from home and floating so free

Twirling, swirling, singing the mermaid song.

Author's Note

OCEANS ARE HUGE, WILD, wonderful places that need our help. Grandpa Siren knows the dangers of oil in the ocean, and I hope you do too. We must do what we can to protect our waters from pollution.

Scientists find new creatures in the ocean all the time. Maybe one day they will find a mermaid! Check out the glossary for some interesting information about oceans and their inhabitants. Write to me on Kids Talk at www.debbiedadey.com and tell me your favorite sea creature.

Take care,
Debbie Dadey

Glossary

BLUE WHALE: The blue whale is the largest animal that has ever lived. Its heart is the size of a car!

CLAM: In real life, the giant clam is usually only five feet wide.

CLEANER SHRIMP: These shrimp clean parasites and bacteria off fish.

CONCH: Sea snail shells are sometimes used for decoration or even for blowing to make noise.

CRAB: The Japanese spider crab is the largest crab and can sometimes live for one hundred years!

CRUSTACEAN: Krill, lobsters, crabs, and shrimp are all part of a group of animals known as crustaceans.

DOGFISH: The piked dogfish is actually a shark. It can live to be one hundred years old.

DOLPHIN: The bottlenose dolphin is known to play with humans in the wild.

EMPEROR SHRIMP: Emperor shrimp live on sea cucumbers.

GLASSWORT: Common glasswort can be eaten. Sometimes it is boiled like asparagus.

GREEN SEA TURTLE: Green sea turtles lay up to two hundred eggs at a time, but their numbers still have dwindled because they are hunted for human food.

HAMMERHEAD SHARK: The strange, broad shape of this shark's head actually helps it in hunting for food.

HARLEQUIN SHRIMP: Somehow these small shrimp are able to work in pairs to catch much larger starfish.

HINGE-BEAK SHRIMP: Some shrimp actually glow!

HUMPBACK WHALE: Male humpback whale songs can be heard from miles away by other humpbacks.

JELLYFISH: The moon jellyfish is the most common of the two hundred types of jellyfish, some of which glow.

KILLER WHALE: The killer whale is not a whale at all, but a dolphin.

KRILL: Antarctic krill are only about two inches long. Krill feed on algae that grow under the ice.

OCTOPUS: The giant octopus changes color to suit its mood. If it's mad, it turns red.

ORANGE SEA PEN: This sea creature looks like an old-fashioned quill pen.

OYSTER AND MUSSEL: Oysters have long been eaten by man, and this has led the common oyster to nearly disappear. Most oysters eaten today are commercially farmed.

PAINTED STINKFISH: Painted stinkfish are colorful and like to bury themselves in the sand.

PLANKTON: Plankton is an organism that cannot swim strongly, so it flows with the currents.

RIBBON WORM: Nemertine worms, also known as "ribbon worms," can grow to be as long as a football field is wide.

SEA CUCUMBER: Sea cucumbers clean up the bottom of the sea.

SEA LILY: Sea lilies live on the seafloor and are similar in many ways to starfish.

SEAWEED: Giant kelp is the largest seaweed. It can grow two feet in one day!

SNAPPING SHRIMP: This tiny creature is only one to two inches long, but its tremendous snapping sound makes it one of the loudest animals in the ocean.

SPONGE: The Mediterranean bath sponge is soft enough to make a cushion!

STARFISH: Starfish are also known as sea stars. Most have five arms, but there is a seven-arm starfish as well as the crown-of-thorns starfish, which has up to twenty arms.

VENT TUBE WORM: Huge worms (as tall as a person) live near hot water vents on the ocean floor.

ZOOPLANKTON: This is animal plankton. Jellyfish are a type of zooplankton.